The Ghost in the Telly

In the middle of the night something disturbed him. Sitting up in bed, yawning sleepily, he stared into the corner of the room and saw that the television screen was fizzing with its usual white and grey snowstorm.

"Who switched that on?" muttered Bill blearily.

Just as he said that the ghostly face appeared on the screen. Bill gasped in fright but before he could utter a word the face shimmered like a mirage and called out.

Collect these other Young Hippo ghost stories, if you dare!

FRANK RODGERS

The Ghost
in the Telly

Illustrated by Philip Hopman

Scholastic Children's Books,
Commonwealth House, 1-19 New Oxford Street,
London WC1A 1NU, UK
a division of Scholastic Ltd
London ~ New York ~ Toronto ~ Sydney ~ Auckland
Mexico City ~ New Delhi ~ Hong Kong

Published in the UK by Scholastic Ltd, 1999

Text copyright © Frank Rodgers, 1999
Illustrations copyright © Philip Hopman, 1999

ISBN 0 590 11398 4

Printed by Cox & Wyman Ltd, Reading, Berks.

2 4 6 8 10 9 7 5 3 1

Chapter 1

It was a wet Sunday evening and Bill was bored. He sat on the edge of his bed feeling glum.

"Nothing to do," he muttered.

He had phoned a few of his pals but they were all busy.

Don't feel like reading, he thought. What I *do* feel like is watching some telly but Mum is hogging the TV right now. She's probably watching a cooking programme or a documentary on something fascinating like *slugs*.

He sighed and looked round his room. "I wish I had a telly of my own," he muttered. "Everyone else has."

There was a tap on the door and Bill's dad popped his head into the room.

"Busy, Bill?"

Bill put his head in his hands. "Bored," he muttered, then he looked up hopefully. "Dad…?" he began for the hundredth time. "I wish I—"

His dad held up a hand. "I know," he said, grinning, "you wish you had a TV of your own. Well, you know we can't afford one."

Bill sighed again. "I know," he said.

"But", his dad went on, a glimmer of fun in his eyes, "I've found one."

Bill jumped off the bed. "You have?"

"I have," beamed his dad. He pushed open the door and came into the bedroom carrying a large cardboard box. Carefully depositing the box on the floor, he reached inside and lifted out a huge TV set.

Bill's heart sank. The TV was ancient. It had a brown wooden casing with plastic knobs on the front that looked like they had come from a toy cooker, and the two-pronged aerial that sat on top reminded Bill of a snail's antennae.

"There," said his dad with a smile. "What do you think? Not bad for a couple of quid, eh?"

Bill tried hard to hide his disappointment. It wasn't exactly what he'd had in mind. He had imagined owning something along the lines of a brand new Sondig UltraScope with teletext and remote control – the kind owned by at least three of his school pals.

"Where did you get it?" he asked.

"You know that Victorian house in Hawthorn Lane, the one the old couple lived in?"

"The old couple that died?"

"Yes. Well, someone else had just moved in and they were selling off some of the stuff from the house down at the market."

"So this TV came from the old house?"

"Yes."

"Does it work?" Bill asked, hoping for one mad moment that his dad would say no and take it away again. The last thing Bill wanted was his pals at school finding out he had a TV that was as ancient as this one. What an embarrassment!

"Oh yes," said his dad brightly and

Bill's heart sank even deeper. "Like a charm. Well," he went on sheepishly, "*almost* like a charm."

"Almost?"

"Yes," said his dad. "Er … sometimes all you get is snow."

"Snow?"

"You know, that white, hissy stuff you see on the screen when the programmes have finished."

Great, thought Bill. Snow. Very Christmassy.

His dad put the set on a table, plugged it in and adjusted the aerial. The picture fizzed a little then settled down.

"There," beamed his dad. "Not bad, is it?"

Bill looked. Fuzzy red and blue

figures ran about against a grainy green background.

"Football!" cried Dad.

"Is it?" said Bill, peering closely. "Oh, so it is."

His dad glanced at him and lifted an eyebrow.

"I'll take it away again if you don't want it, Bill," he said, sounding slightly offended.

Bill sighed. "No. It's OK, Dad. It's fine, thanks. I'm sure I'll get a better picture if I adjust the aerial a bit more."

"That's the spirit!" said Dad cheerfully. "Happy watching!" And with that he left the bedroom.

Bill watched the fuzzy football for a few more seconds, then tried to adjust the picture. As he moved the aerial, however, the picture vanished and in its place was a snowstorm.

"Oh, great!" muttered Bill, fiddling with the aerial. But it didn't seem to matter where he put it as the screenful of hissing snow didn't change.

"Oh, great!" he said again and, disgustedly, reached out to switch off the set. But just as his fingers touched the Off button something happened to make him snatch his hand away. The thousands and thousands of tiny white

dots on the screen suddenly swarmed together and formed the shape of a face – a wobbly, grainy, ghostly face staring at him.

Bill stared back at it uneasily. He'd never seen anything like it before. It was creepy.

Perhaps I'll get the football back if I switch the set off and then on again, he thought. Gingerly he reached out and turned the Off button. He heard the *click* as the set was switched off then stared in disbelief. The face was still there!

Bill stared harder then gasped and backed off slightly. The face seemed to be moving. The eyes blinked and the mouth opened as if it was about to say something.

"Bill…" it whispered. "Help…"

That was enough. With a yelp of panic Bill leapt to the wall socket and yanked out the plug.

The face disappeared.

Panting with relief, Bill stared wide-eyed at the blank screen for a few seconds then began to edge towards the door. I have to tell Dad about this, he said to himself, but then stopped. I can't do that, he thought miserably. He'll just think I'm complaining about the old telly. Over his fright now, he slouched across the room to his bed and sat down again, staring at the dark screen.

"Maybe I just imagined it all," he muttered hopefully. "Yes … maybe." But he kept on sitting on his bed looking at the TV set. He just didn't have the nerve to get up and switch it back on again.

Chapter 2

On his way to school next day Bill met Simon, one of his pals, and before he could stop himself he told him what had happened.

Simon looked at him, grinning in disbelief. "It *said* something?" he chortled. "Your telly spoke to you? Called you by your name after you switched it off?"

Bill suddenly felt very foolish. He didn't know why he had told Simon about it. He had almost convinced himself that it hadn't happened and had vowed to himself that he wouldn't tell anyone. But somehow he had just blurted it out.

"Er … yeah, it said 'help' – or it might even have been 'hello', I'm not sure which," Bill went on miserably. "The voice was just as fuzzy as the face."

Simon's grin became wider. "As fuzzy as your brain, you mean, Bill. Talking telly? Come off it!" And he let out a great guffaw.

Bill wanted to go on, explain how he felt. But he didn't. He knew that Simon would laugh even more so he just grinned sheepishly and said,

"Yeah, you're right, Simon. I probably just imagined it all."

"Why don't you ask your parents to buy you a decent TV?" Simon said. "A new one instead of one that's a hundred years old."

Bill scowled. He hated admitting to anyone that his parents couldn't afford it.

"It would be nice to have a new one," he said with as much dignity as he could, "but it's really not that important."

Simon shrugged. "Fair enough," he said and changed the subject. "By the way, have you seen the new boy in our class?"

"New boy?" said Bill. "Since when?"

"He arrived on Friday when you were at the dentist's," said Simon. "Mrs Halliday has put him next to you."

"Yeah? What's he like?"

"Seems OK," said Simon.

Bill nodded and groaned inwardly. He wasn't looking forward to meeting someone new. He always found it hard to think of something to say.

But Bill was surprised. Mel Briggs,

the new boy in the class, was the sunniest character he had ever met – and so easy to talk to! By the end of the day, to Bill's amazement, they were chatting away nineteen to the dozen as if they had known each other all their lives.

"Where do you live?" asked Bill as they walked home together after school.

Mel smiled. "My parents have this thing about do-it-yourself, Bill," he said, "so they looked for a house they could renovate. They found one in Hawthorn Lane. It's in a bit of a state but that's what they wanted." He laughed. "You should see them. They can't wait to start painting and decorating! And I'll get roped in too, of course."

Bill stared. "Hawthorn Lane? So *you*'re the ones that have moved into the old house? The one that used to be owned by the old couple that died?"

Mel nodded. "That's right, Mr and Mrs Smiley. My mum and dad cleared out a lot of their stuff – mostly useless old junk – and sold it at the market. Although," he grinned, "there are still lots of bits and pieces left in a room in the basement – old chairs, tables, a wardrobe and even an old bed. It's like a little house all in one room."

Bill felt embarrassed. How could he tell Mel that he had one of those bits of "old junk" in his bedroom? He resolved there and then to throw the TV into the bin as soon as he got home.

Then Mel surprised him with a strange question.

"Do you believe in ghosts, Bill?" he asked thoughtfully.

Bill remembered the strange face he had seen on the TV screen.

"I'm not sure," he replied slowly.

Mel nodded. "I think I do," he said. "Since last night."

"You saw a ghost?"

Mel shook his head. "No, I didn't *see* it … but I *heard* it."

"What happened?" Bill asked eagerly.

"It was creepy," said Mel softly. "I woke up in the middle of the night and heard a voice outside my door. I thought it said, 'Where is he?' so I got up and opened the door. I thought it was Mum – it sounded like a woman's voice – and I wondered what was going on. But," he looked at Bill, his eyes wide, "there was no one there."

"Perhaps it was your mum and she had just gone back to bed," suggested Bill.

Mel shook his head and gave a quick smile.

"No, it wasn't her," he said.

"Burglars?" said Bill with a frown.

Mel shook his head again.

"No," he said, "it wasn't that either because just then I heard footsteps coming along the hall towards me … and the hall was empty!

Bill stared, open mouthed.

"What did you do?"

"I was frozen to the spot," said Mel. "Scared stiff. I didn't know what to do.

The footsteps came up to me, passed me and carried on along the hall. I felt a coldness as they went by, then they just sort of faded away."

"Phew!" muttered Bill. "Spooky."

"It sure was," said Mel. "I ran in and told Mum and Dad about it but they said I had probably dreamed it – that perhaps I had been sleep-walking. So I just went back to bed and when I woke up this morning it certainly seemed like a dream. I almost convinced myself that the whole thing hadn't happened. Isn't that daft?"

Bill shook his head and thought of his old television set.

"No," he said. "I don't think it sounds daft at all, Mel."

Chapter 3

That evening Bill went shopping for old Mrs Hegarty who lived next door. Then he did his paper round, helped his dad patch some of the rusty holes in their old car, and finished his homework. By the time he got upstairs he was so tired he went straight to bed.

"You're going tomorrow," he

muttered at the television set, yawning. "Definitely." Then he turned over and fell asleep.

In the middle of the night something disturbed him. Sitting up in bed, yawning sleepily, he stared into the corner of the room and saw that the television screen was fizzing with its usual white and grey snowstorm.

"Who switched that on?" muttered Bill blearily.

Just as he said that the ghostly face appeared on the screen. Bill gasped in fright but before he could utter a word the face shimmered like a mirage and called out.

"Don't yell, Bill," it said. "Your parents might not understand."

Bill nearly fell out of bed with shock.

He stared, speechless, but after a few seconds he found his voice and stammered, "What – how – who are you?"

The fuzz of dots on the screen wavered again then packed themselves together more tightly until the face resolved itself into that of a kindly old man.

"I'm Alf Smiley," said the face. "I used to live in Hawthorn Lane."

"B-b-but you're *dead*," stuttered Bill.

"Of course. I'm a ghost," replied Alf Smiley reasonably.

Bill closed his eyes and swallowed hard. "This is all a dream," he told himself. "When I open my eyes the TV will be off and the ghost will be gone." He counted to three and opened his eyes again.

The ghost was still there.

"I heard your dad mention your name last night," said Alf. "That's why I know who you are. I tried to talk to you but you switched me off. Pulled out the plug."

"But…" said Bill slowly, pointing at the socket, "the plug's out now!"

Alf Smiley smiled. "It took me a little while to find out I could use my own energy to create a picture on the screen. It's very tiring but I can do it."

Bill couldn't believe it. Here he was, talking to a ghost in his telly.

He got out of bed and sat on the edge warily.

"So," he said, "what are you doing in the TV? I didn't know that ghosts haunted tellies."

"They don't," said Alf ruefully. "It's just that I used to like mending things. I never got around to fixing this old telly when I was alive, so when I became a ghost I thought I'd give it a try."

"What happened?" asked Bill.

"Well," said Alf rather shamefacedly, "I went inside the TV one night to have a bit of a poke about, then before I knew what was happening, someone had taken the set out of the house and sold it to your dad!"

"Can't you just ... er ... *fly* back to Hawthorn Lane?" asked Bill.

"I'm afraid not," said Alf. "I'm

trapped in here. The electricity inside the TV has sucked up a lot of my energy and now I don't have enough strength to get out of the cathode ray tube. It feels like I'm fading away but I should be all right as long as nobody tampers with the set."

"What do you mean?" asked Bill.

"Well," answered Alf grimly, "if anybody tried to improve the picture quality by adjusting the controls at the back of the set it could be the end of me. The surge of electricity would scramble me like eggs in a mixer and break me up into tiny particles of energy. I'd be stuck inside this telly for ever!"

Bill gulped. "That's terrible," he said.

"It certainly is," replied Alf. "The

only way I'll get out in one piece is if the TV is taken back to the house in Hawthorn Lane – soon. My wife might be able to help me. She's got lots of energy, you see," he said proudly, "and she could boost mine so I could break free."

"Your wife?"

"Oh yes," smiled Alf. "My dear old Florence. We liked the old house so much when we lived there that we decided to come back and stay in it as ghosts." Suddenly he looked sad. "I miss her a lot," he said, "and she'll be missing me. You see, Flo and I have never ever been apart for more than a few hours and she'll be worried sick about me. She won't know what has happened and will probably be searching the house."

Bill gasped. "She is!" he cried. "A friend of mine and his family have moved into your old house, Alf. Last night Mel heard a voice and footsteps. He was sure it was a ghost."

"Oh dear," groaned Alf. "That would have been Florence looking for

me. What can I do? Can you help? If you could just take this old telly back to Hawthorn Lane..."

Bill frowned. "I don't know if they'll want to have it back, Alf. But I'll ask Mel. I'm sure we'll manage something."

"Oh, I'm so relieved," said Alf. "Now, if you don't mind I'll have a rest. I've used up a lot of energy and I'm dead tired."

Bill smiled. He couldn't imagine anyone being more dead tired than Alf.

"OK, Alf," he said. "I'll speak to you after school tomorrow. All right?"

"Fine," sighed Alf, his face fading. "Fine."

The screen went blank.

It was a long time before Bill got back to sleep. As he lay in the dark and thought about his haunted telly

he felt excited shivers run up and down his spine. He had decided to keep what had happened a secret from his parents just for the moment – but he couldn't wait to tell Mel!

Chapter 4

Bill caught up with Mel just as he was going through the school gates next morning. But before he could tell him about Alf, Mel began talking excitedly.

"It was amazing last night, Bill," he said. "Even scarier than the night before! About two o'clock in the morning we were all woken up by the sound of doors banging. Mum and Dad and I rushed out of our bedrooms and looked down into the hall and we all saw the living-room door close by itself! Then we heard footsteps crossing the hall and saw the kitchen door open and shut. A moment later it opened and shut again with a bang and the footsteps went back across the hall. And then," said Mel, his eyes wide, "we heard the voice, all quivery and shaky. 'Where are you?' it said. 'Where are you?'" Mel shook his head, his usually cheery face solemn. "I'm telling you, Bill, it was a real chiller. I was covered in goosebumps. It felt like the ghost was looking for us!" He shook his head again. "I still can't believe it. A ghost!

I live in a haunted house!"

"I know," said Bill.

Mel looked at him. "What do you mean, you know?" he asked suspiciously. Then he grinned. "You don't really believe me, do you?"

"As a matter of fact I do," replied Bill, smiling. "I've been talking to a ghost myself."

"You're having me on, aren't you?" asked Mel. "You're winding me up."

"No," protested Bill, "I'm not. Honest! I was about to tell you but I couldn't get a word in edgeways.'

Mel grinned and shrugged. "OK, so I'll shut up. Tell me."

"You remember you told me your dad had sold some of the junk from your house?" said Bill.

"Yes."

Bill looked a bit sheepish and hesitated. He still didn't like the idea of telling someone, even Mel, about the old TV. "I … er … that is … well, my dad bought me the old telly that your dad got rid of."

"That old thing?" said Mel. "Why?"

Well, thought Bill, I may as well get it over with. He took a deep breath. "It's just," he said, "that he's a bit broke since he was made redundant. It's all he could afford."

To his surprise and relief Mel nodded.

"I know what it's like," he said. "My dad was unemployed for ages. It wasn't much fun. Still, possessions aren't everything, as my mum says."

Bill felt as if a weight had been lifted off him. Mel understood!

"So," Mel went on, "what were you saying about the telly?"

"Alf Smiley's inside it!" Bill blurted out.

"What? Mr Smiley? The old man that used to live in my house?"

Bill nodded and Mel stared at him strangely before asking, "What do you mean he's *inside* the TV?"

Bill looked around to see if anyone could overhear but everyone else in the playground was busy doing their own thing.

"He's a ghost," he hissed. "The husband of the old lady that's haunting your house."

Mel stared at him again, understanding dawning on his face.

"True?" he gasped.

Bill nodded. "True," he said, and explained what had happened.

When he had finished Mel whistled softly. "This is serious, Bill," he said. "We've got to bring the old telly back to my house so that Flo can add her energy to Alf's. It's the only way that Alf will have a chance of being set free. And it's the only chance my family has got of stopping Flo from being so noisy every night. I think I'd rather be haunted by a nice, happy, quiet old couple than one noisy, lonely old lady."

Bill grinned. "That's settled, then," he said. "We'll fetch the telly from my house right after school."

"You're on," said Mel.

Chapter 5

"This is Mel, Mum. My friend from school," said Bill as he and Mel came into the kitchen.

Bill's mum turned from the pot she was stirring on the cooker and smiled. "Nice to meet you, Mel," she said. "How is your new house?"

"Noisy, Mrs Martin," said Mel.

"Especially at night."

He shared a quick grin with Bill as they left the kitchen and heard Bill's mum mutter, puzzled, "Noisy at night? But I thought Hawthorn Lane was the quietest street in town."

The boys hurried upstairs and went into Bill's bedroom.

"The telly's in here, Mel," said Bill, then stopped so suddenly that Mel bumped into him.

"You need brake lights!" said Mel with a laugh, giving him a gentle push in the back.

Bill hardly reacted. "It's gone," he said in amazement, pointing to the empty table by the bookcase. "It was there when I left this morning."

"Perhaps your mother moved it,"

suggested Mel.

"I doubt it," Bill replied, but he searched the room just in case. "No," he said at last, "it's not in here."

"You don't think," said Mel slowly, "that old Alf could have somehow summoned up enough energy to ... er ... *fly* the TV set back to Hawthorn Lane?"

"I doubt it," said Bill. "Anyway, don't you think my parents might have noticed a blooming great telly floating down the stairs?"

"You're right," said Mel.

"I'll ask Mum," muttered Bill worriedly. "She's *got* to know where it is."

"I hope she does," said Mel. "If she doesn't we're in trouble."

They rushed downstairs and burst into the kitchen.

"Where's that old telly gone, Mum?" cried Bill. "It's not in my room. Have you or Dad moved it?"

His mum looked apologetic. "Oh, yes, sorry, Bill," she said. "I forgot to tell you. Your dad took it down to Mr Pipe's repair shop." She smiled. "He felt a bit guilty that the picture was so bad and thought Mr Pipe might be able to fix it."

"What? Oh, no!" wailed Bill. "I wanted it just the way it was! Come on, Mel!" he cried, and both of them rushed out of the house leaving Bill's mum looking puzzled again.

"I thought he'd be pleased," she said as the door slammed.

"Keep your fingers crossed that Mr Pipe hasn't tried to repair the telly, Mel," panted Bill as they ran along the road. "If he has then Alf is done for. He'll be stuck in that telly for ever."

"And if he's stuck in the telly then we're stuck with Flo banging about at all hours of the night," replied Mel breathlessly.

Mr Pipe's electrical repair shop looked just like a junk shop. The window was full of second-hand appliances with yellowing price tags and faded display cards and the inside of the shop was just as full as the window. It was crammed with old TV sets, videos, record players, kettles, irons, toasters, vacuum cleaners and clocks. It was as if people had brought their things in to be repaired and had then forgotten all about them.

A little bell tinkled as Bill and Mel pushed open the door. Mr Pipe was nowhere in sight.

"He's probably in his repair room at the back," said Bill and called out, "Mr Pipe! Shop!"

Mr Pipe appeared almost immediately from a door half-hidden behind a fridge-freezer at the back of the shop. He was a little man with bright red cheeks and a sharp nose and always reminded Bill of a robin.

"What can I do you for, lads?" he asked, wiping his oily hands on a rag.

"My dad brought in an old TV set to be repaired, Mr Pipe," Bill began.

Mr Pipe adjusted his wire-rimmed glasses and peered at him.

"Ah! Young Bill," he said. "Didn't recognize you for a moment. What was it you said?"

"The old TV, Mr Pipe. Have you done anything with it yet?"

Mr Pipe shook his head.

"Didn't take me two seconds to see that the old telly was a goner, Bill. Not worth repairing, that one. So your dad's thinking about buying another one for you."

"He is?" Bill exclaimed. He felt terrible. He knew his dad couldn't afford it and was only doing this because he had seen how disappointed Bill was with the old telly.

"So," Mel asked anxiously, "where's

Bill's telly now, Mr Pipe?"

Mr Pipe waved a hand vaguely. "Er … it's out the back, I think. In the yard. It's in a pile with some others waiting for the scrapman to take them away."

"Scrapman?" Bill and Mel yelped together.

"Can we look and see if it's still there?" Bill pleaded. "We'd like it back."

"Of course," said Mr Pipe. "Go up the lane at the side of the shop and into the yard by the back gate. If it's still there then take it away by all means."

"Thanks!" The boys rushed out, leaving Mr Pipe scratching his head in puzzlement, muttering, "I thought he'd be pleased to be rid of the old thing."

Bill and Mel tumbled through the back gate to Mr Pipe's yard and looked around frantically. The yard was empty.

Mr Pipe popped his head round his back door and shrugged. "Sorry, lads," he said mournfully. "Looks like the scrapman has taken the lot. Pity."

"Which scrapman was it?" cried Bill.

"Tim Ferris, Copper Lane," replied Mr Pipe. "Know where that is?"

"Yes!" yelled Bill, and he turned and bolted out of the yard with Mel in hot pursuit.

"Poor Alf!" gasped Bill as they pounded along the pavement. "He's safe for the moment but he'll be getting weaker – fading away to nothing. Poor Flo might never be able to find him. She'll wander round your house looking for him for ever."

"Yeah, and poor us," muttered Mel, panting. "No sleep for the rest of our lives!"

Chapter 6

Five minutes later the boys turned the corner into Copper Lane and dashed up the cobbled street towards Tim Ferris's yard at the other end. When they got there they found that the tall wooden gates were locked.

Bill rattled the gate and shouted, "Mr Ferris! Mr Ferris!" But no one appeared.

"He's not here," groaned Mel. "What do we do now?"

"Look!" cried Bill, pointing into the yard between the slats in the gate. "It's the telly!"

By the back door of the office, almost hidden by all the other scrap in the yard, was a pile of TV sets. On top of it was Bill's television.

Mel looked at Bill. "Let's go get it!" he cried, grinning.

"You mean ... climb over?" asked Bill.

"Sure!" Mel retorted. "Of course! Come on!" And with that he began to climb the gate.

Bill grinned too. "Wait for me!" he called and started up after Mel.

Although the gate was tall it was easy to climb and a few seconds later they dropped down into the yard and ran over to the pile of TV sets.

Bill saw, to his relief, that the old television set didn't look too damaged. There was a scrape or two on the wood veneer but that was all.

"I hope Alf is OK," he said anxiously.

At that the screen flickered into life

and Alf's face appeared in the fizzy snow.

Mel gasped and pointed.

"It's… It's…" he stammered.

Bill grinned in relief. "It's just Alf," he said. He bent down and peered at the screen. "Alf, meet Mel."

"Hello, Mel," said Alf, his voice sounding crackly and distant. "Have you come to take me home?"

Mel gulped and smiled. "We certainly have, Alf," he said.

"So just hold on a bit longer, all right?" said Bill.

"I'll try, Bill," said Alf, "but I feel the electricity in the set is gradually taking me over. I'm getting weaker and weaker."

"Oh, no!" gasped Bill. "Switch off, then," he suggested quickly. "Save your strength, Alf."

"Righty-ho," said Alf and his face faded away again.

"Wow!" breathed Mel. "Wow!"

"Time for Operation Save-a-Ghost!" said Bill.

"Right!" said Mel.

The boys heaved the old TV set off the pile and carried it to the gate.

"How are we going to get it over?" muttered Bill. "It weighs a tonne!"

"I'll climb to the top," said Mel, "and you heave it up to me. I'll balance it on the top of the gate and you can climb over. Then I'll pass it down to you."

"Fair enough," agreed Bill.

But as Mel began to climb the gate they heard a fearsome barking behind them. They whirled round and saw an enormous black dog run round the side of the office and rush towards them, snarling.

"Help! gasped Mel, scrambling to the top of the gate. "Jump, Bill! Jump!"

Leaving the TV, Bill jumped. He

grasped hold of the gate with one hand and Mel's outstretched hand with the other and somehow managed to climb up beside Mel before the dog reached him. He and Mel sat astride the top and felt the gate shake as the dog threw itself against it, barking furiously.

"Whew!" gasped Bill. "Close shave!"

"Sure was," said Mel, then both of them had to clutch the top slat to prevent themselves falling off as the gate shook violently again. "What now?"

"No idea," replied Bill glumly. "We're stuck. I'd better tell Alf." He called down to the TV set. "Alf! Alf!"

This provoked the dog into another round of frenzied barking. It leapt against the gate, yellow teeth bared, snarling and baying as the boys clung on tightly. Then suddenly it stopped and stared at the TV set. It backed off slightly, haunches quivering, jaws dripping.

"What's going on?" muttered Mel. Then he realized that the dog was

looking at the screen which had begun to fizz again.

"It's Alf," said Bill. "He's speaking."

They listened and heard Alf say, "I'm going to try something, lads. It's the only way out of here. Get off the gate and wait for me on the other side. You might even have to catch me."

"Catch?" cried Bill as he and Mel climbed down. "What are you going to do, jump?"

"Fly, I hope," said Alf. "I think I might just have enough energy left."

The black dog was becoming bolder. It edged towards the TV set, a low growl starting deep in its throat.

"Here goes," said Alf.

The dog stopped with a jerk and its eyes widened. A moment later its tail went between its legs as the TV set began to shake … and slowly lift off the ground. The animal took one more look and, yelping in fright, turned and bolted. Bill and Mel watched in amazement as the television slowly and shakily rose into the air until it was just above the top of the gate.

It hovered there uncertainly for a few seconds and Bill muttered, "Come on, Alf, you can do it!"

The television gave a little shake and slowly began to float down towards them.

"Yes!" cried Mel.

"You can do it, Alf!" exclaimed Bill.

They both reached up, straining to get a grip on the set as it came within reach. But as Bill felt his fingertips touch the bottom of the casing he heard Alf gasp.

"I can't … hold on … any more!" he wheezed, and suddenly the television dropped out of the air.

"Aaaargh!" yelped Bill. "Catch it, Mel!"

"I'm trying to!" cried Mel as they both reached up frantically to steady the heavy set as it fell towards the ground. Their combined efforts managed to break the set's fall, but they couldn't hold on to it. With cries of dismay they felt it slip out of their grasp and hit the ground with a crunching smack.

"Oh, no!" wailed Bill, and he and Mel got down on their hands and knees beside the television set.

"Alf!" Bill cried. "Alf!"

There was no reply. The screen stayed blank.

"What's happened to him?" groaned Mel.

Quickly they examined the set. The corner was crumpled where it had struck the ground, the casing was split and there was a crack right across the screen.

"Doesn't look too good," breathed Bill worriedly.

"And it could be damaged inside," said Mel.

Bill looked at him miserably. "Poor Alf," he said quietly. "I hope we still have a chance of saving him."

"Come on," said Mel grimly. "We mustn't give up. Let's get it back to my house."

"Right," replied Bill, helping Mel lift the set up. "If we can get it back to Hawthorn Lane his wife might still be able to help him."

Carefully carrying the set between them they hurried off up the lane.

Chapter 7

Mel's parents were fascinated when they heard what had happened.

"Unbelievable!" muttered his dad as he examined the old TV set that the boys had deposited on the floor. "Just think, there's a ghost in there!"

"What can we do?" asked his mum.

"Not much, I'm afraid, Mrs Briggs,"

said Bill. "We'll just have to hope that Alf's wife, Florence, appears and is able to help him. Where did you find the TV set when you moved in?"

"It was in that little room in the basement, Mum, wasn't it?" said Mel. He turned to Bill. "Remember I told you about it, Bill. The one with all the furniture in it?"

Bill nodded. "Maybe that's where they were planning to stay as ghosts," he suggested.

"Yes," murmured Mel's mum. "I think you're right, Bill. It's like a cosy little bed-sit."

"I wish I'd left the old set where it was," said Mel's dad. "What a lot of trouble I caused!"

"Don't blame yourself, dear," said his

wife. "Perhaps if we put it back now it would help."

"You're right," said Mel's father. "Let's do it." He hefted the set into his arms and everyone followed him down the stairs to the basement. He put the set down carefully on a table against the wall and stood back.

Bill looked around at the two comfortable chairs on either side of the fireplace in the kitchen range, the lace-covered table and the old pictures on the wall.

"That's them!" he said suddenly, pointing to a faded framed photograph of Alf and Florence on their wedding day. "I recognize Alf."

Everyone looked.

"Oh, isn't that sweet?" said Mel's mum. "They look such a lovely couple." She glanced around and pointed to the old cast-iron cooking range. "It must have been so warm and cosy in here that they made this room into their parlour and forgot about the rest of the house. I can just see them sitting in their chairs in front of that little fireplace, enjoying each other's company." She sighed.

"Well, dear," said her husband, "if Alf manages to get out of that telly then he and Florence can stay here as long as they like."

Bill grinned. "I'm sure they'd love that, Mr Briggs," he said and patted the TV set. "Did you hear that, Alf?" he whispered softly.

Everyone looked at the screen but it remained blank. It then occurred to Bill that he should plug the set in and switch it on, but that didn't make any difference. The television remained silent.

"The insides must have been damaged in the fall after all," groaned Mel.

Bill nodded slowly, then turned to Mel's parents.

"Would you mind if I stayed around for a bit, Mr and Mrs Briggs?" he asked. "I'd like to see if Alf makes it or not."

"Of course, Bill," said Mrs Briggs. "In fact," she went on, "why don't you phone your mum and dad and ask them to come over for some supper? I'm sure they'd like to know what's going on too."

Bill's mum and dad were delighted to be asked, but when they arrived it took them a little while to get used to the fact that the house was haunted.

"Are you sure about all this, Bill?" asked his dad softly for the tenth time.

"Oh yes, I'm sure, Dad," said Bill. "Alf is definitely in that old telly. Just keep your fingers crossed that his wife can help him, that's all."

That evening everybody took it in turns to keep watch in the little room, but nothing happened.

Both sets of parents took to each other right away and found they had lots of things in common. They liked the same kinds of films and TV shows and had even been to the same seaside resort for their holidays. Also, Mel's dad had once worked as a joiner, like Bill's dad.

"Sorry to hear you've been made redundant, Jim," he said. "But I know a chap who has a joinery business and he's looking for workers just now.

Maybe you could give him a ring."

Bill's dad smiled. "I'll do that, Sam," he said. "Thanks."

Bill smiled wryly. At least some things seemed to be working out well, he thought.

Chapter 8

The evening wore on and it got dark but still nothing had happened. Neither Alf nor Flo had made an appearance.

By now everyone was crowded into the little room, gazing at the silent TV set.

"Oh dear," said Bill's mum softly to

him. "I hope poor old Alf is still all right and that Florence can find him in time. I mean, she doesn't even know he's inside the telly, does she?"

Just as she said this, however, the lights in the room flickered and became dimmer. At the same moment everyone started as they heard the noise of a door banging in the room above followed by footsteps on the stairs.

"Where are you?" called a trembly voice. "Alf … where are you?"

The door opened by itself and a gust of cold air rushed into the room, making everyone shiver and huddle together.

Suddenly the ghostly form of an old lady appeared beside them and they all gasped in surprise.

"It's her!" whispered Bill. "It's Florence!" and everyone gazed at her in amazement as she shimmered in front of them like a hologram.

Florence was a small woman with white hair tied up in a bun at the back of her head and she wore a long dress with a frilly collar. Bill could see that her kindly face was lined with worry as she looked round the room.

"Where are you, Alf?" the ghost asked softly in a voice like a sighing wind. "Are you in here?"

The old television screen began to glow and everyone heard a faint hissing noise.

"Look!" whispered Bill and Mel. "It's Alf."

A faint, wavery image appeared among the snowy dots.

"Flo…"

Alf's voice was so thin and faint that at first Bill thought he had imagined it.

But there was a gasp from Flo and she moved forward to peer at the TV.

"Alf…" she said, unsure, "is that you? Are you inside this old telly?"

"Yes." Alf's voice was barely above a whisper.

"Oh Alf," cried Flo. "I've been looking for you everywhere. I thought I'd lost you for ever."

"No," said Alf. "I'm here, old dear. But I'm very weak, Flo. I've almost faded away to nothing and I can't get out. I'm trapped."

Flo shook her head and smiled fondly and brushed away a ghostly tear.

"How many times have I told you, Alf Smiley, about poking your nose in where it's not wanted?"

"Sorry, Flo," said Alf.

"Don't worry, Alf," said Flo. "I'm going to try and help you. Move over – I'm coming in."

The old lady drifted into the air above the TV set and everyone held their breath. Then, like smoke pouring in reverse, she vanished inside the TV.

Bill and Mel and their parents gathered round expectantly.

"Do you think she'll manage it?" Bill asked Mel.

Mel grinned. "Flo looks like a very determined old lady. Yes, I think she'll do it."

But long minutes passed and nothing happened.

Just as everyone thought that Flo was stuck inside the TV too, it began to shake.

"Move back, everybody," said Mel's dad.

Bill felt his mother's hands on his

shoulders pulling him towards the door as everyone moved away uneasily.

The TV was now shaking so much it had rattled itself across the table and was teetering on the edge.

"Watch out!" yelled Bill suddenly. "It's going over!"

Everyone gasped and watched as, almost in slow motion, the old television toppled off the edge of the table and fell to the floor. It hit the edge of the fireplace and burst open, sending a plume of smoke into the air.

There was silence in the room as everyone gaped at the shattered remains of the TV set and the grey cloud that hung in the air above.

"Oh, no!" wailed Bill's mum. "The

poor ghosts – they didn't make it!"

Bill suddenly gasped. "Yes they did! Look!" he cried and pointed excitedly at the cloud of smoke. "That's not smoke at all. It's them! It's Alf and Flo! They did make it after all!"

Everyone gasped in delight as they watched the drifting smoke slowly separate into two distinct shapes that floated down to land on the carpet. It was Alf and Flo, smiling and holding hands.

"She did it!" cried Bill. "Flo did it!"

Alf turned to look at them as they all came forward.

"She certainly did," he said, puffing out his chest proudly and sticking his thumb in the pocket of his waistcoat as he surveyed the room. "My old Flo didn't let me down. She's always had a strong personality, you know. And, as I've always said, she's got enough energy for the both of us!"

As everyone laughed and clapped Flo said, "Yes, Alf Smiley. And from now on you'll stay put where I can keep an eye on you!"

Alf turned to Mel's parents.

"I seem to remember you saying that Flo and I would be welcome to stay here," he said. "In this little room?"

Mr and Mrs Briggs nodded.

"We'd be delighted," said Mel's mum.

"Make yourselves at home!" said Mel's dad.

"Thank you!" said Alf and Flo. "And," said Alf, "a specially huge thank-you to Bill and Mel for bringing

me back home!"

"Yes," said Flo. "Will you promise to come and visit us often, boys?"

Bill and Mel nodded. "You bet!" they said.

Alf and Flo settled down in their armchairs by the fire.

"Ah," said Alf. "This is just like old times, my dear."

Flo smiled at Mel's mum and dad.

"From now on I'll be as quiet as a mouse," she said.

* * *

After that the families saw a lot of each other and Bill and Mel became best friends. They went swimming, played football and tennis, read books, and went to the movies together. Bill's dad got the new job and later that year, when Bill's birthday came around, he offered to buy Bill a brand new television.

But Bill shook his head.

"No thanks, Dad," he said. "If you don't mind I'd rather have a bike. Mel and I want to go exploring. Now that we're on friendly terms with two ghosts we want to go and check out old castles and haunted houses to see if we can find any more!" He grinned. "You know," he went on, "I just don't seem to have much time to watch TV these days!"

The End